The Tortoise and the Eagle

Based on a fable by Aesop
Retold by Rob Lloyd Jones

Illustrated by
Eugenia Nobati

Reading Consultant: Alison Kelly
Roehampton University

This is a story about
a tortoise.

He had everything a
tortoise could want.

He had a lovely log
to sit on,

juicy apples
to eat

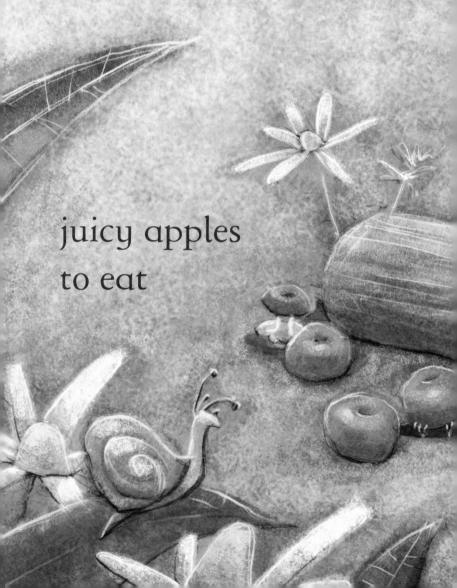

and a very
shiny shell.

But he wasn't happy.

All day long, he saw
an eagle in the sky.

Flying
low.

Flying high.

It had golden feathers
and great big wings.

7

He climbed
onto a rock...

jumped into
the air...

and flopped
onto his belly.

He climbed
up a tree...

jumped into
the air...

and landed splat
in a puddle.

11

He called to the eagle.

"Will you take me into the sky? I want to be like you."

"What will you
give me?" the
eagle replied.

13

"You can have my log and my apples."

"Very well," said the eagle. "I will take you into the sky."

Up and up
the eagle rose...

...up through the clouds
to the bright blue sky.

The tortoise looked
at the ground.

It was a very
long way down.

He felt dizzy. "Eagle," he said. "I don't like it up here."

So the eagle took
the tortoise back to
the ground.

"Little tortoise," said the eagle. "You have no feathers and no wings."

"You're not made for flying."

"Keep your apples and
your log."

"Be happy."

The tortoise smiled. He watched the eagle go.

He ate
his apples.

He sat on his log.

And he no longer
wanted to fly.

PUZZLES

Puzzle 1
Put the pictures in order.

A

B

C

D

E

F

Puzzle 2

Choose three words to describe the tortoise, and three to describe the eagle.

high	running	watching
low	hopping	flying
wet	angry	golden
pink	noisy	sitting

Puzzles 3
Find these things
in the picture:

log   eagle   tortoise
snail   mouse   squirrel

Answers to puzzles

Puzzle 1

C   F   E

A   D   B

Puzzle 2

Eagle:
high
flying
golden

Tortoise:
low
watching
sitting

eagle

bird

tortoise

log

mouse

snail squirrel

About the story

The Tortoise and the Eagle is one of Aesop's Fables, a collection of stories first told in Ancient Greece around 4,000 years ago. The stories always have a "moral" (a message or lesson) at the end. In this story, the tortoise learns to be happy with who he is.

Designed by Michelle Lawrence
Additional design by Emily Bornoff
Series designer: Russell Punter
Series editor: Lesley Sims

First published in 2009 by Usborne Publishing Ltd., Usborne House,
83-85 Saffron Hill, London EC1N 8RT, England. www.usborne.com
Copyright © 2009 Usborne Publishing Ltd.